LIBRARY OF DOOM

THE FINAL CHAPTERS

DEATH SENTENCE

By Michael Dahl

Illustrated by
Nelson Evergreen

raintree

a Capstone company — publishers for children

Raintree is an imprint of Capstone Global Library Limited, a company incorporated in England and Wales having its registered office at 7 Pilgrim Street, London, EC4V 6LB – Registered company number: 6695582

www.raintree.co.uk
myorders@raintree.co.uk

Designed by Hilary Wacholz
Printed and bound in China by Nordica
0914/CA21401556
ISBN 978-1-406-29452-1
18 17 16 15 14
10 9 8 7 6 5 4 3 2 1

British Library Cataloguing in Publication Data
A full catalogue record for this book is available from the British Library.

These are the last days of the Library of Doom.

The forces of villainy are freeing the Library's most dangerous books. Only one thing can stop Evil from penning history's final chapter – the League of Librarians, a mysterious collection of heroes who only appear when the Library faces its greatest threat.

With some books, what you can't see *can* hurt you...

TABLE OF CONTENTS

Chapter 1

SENTENCED

"The best book," says Barnaby, "is a **magic** book."

"The new one I'm reading now is about this blind wizard who –" Barnaby begins.

A tall boy on the bus points at Barnaby and **sneers**. "The Harry Potter nerd wants a magic book!" says the boy.

Barnaby looks up at the boy.

"We are having a private conversation, Adam," Barnaby says.

Adam laughs. "You and your **weird** little friends?" he says.

Adam grabs the book from Barnaby's hands.

"Let's see if your magic book can fly, nerd!"
yells Adam.

He tosses the book towards the back of the
bus.

It lands on the damp metal floor with a
thud.

Barnaby frowns and gets up from his seat.

He **squeezes** past elbows and knees that stick into the aisle.

Jenna, Barnaby's friend, juts her chin towards Adam.

"You are gross!" she says.

Barnaby **reaches** the back of the bus.

He kneels down and finds his new book under the back seat.

Another book lies next to it. It looks old and used.

Barnaby grabs that one too.

A simple title is etched on the dark purple cover:

DEATH SENTENCE

When Barnaby walks back to his seat, Adam takes the old book.

"This one's **not** yours!" says Adam.

Adam opens the book.

"What kind of stupid book is this?" he says.
"There aren't any words!"

He flips through page after page.

They are all blank.

Except for one.

"Finally," says Adam. "A sentence."

And as he reads it to himself, he **disappears**.

The old book falls to the floor of the bus, out of sight.

No one on the bus notices that Adam is gone.

"Why is your new book all **wet** and **dirty**?" asks Jenna.

"Weird," says Barnaby. "I don't know."

Chapter 2

SLIDING

The bus driver **grimly** stares straight ahead.

The route twists and turns through the streets.

At each new turn, the old book slides across the slippery bus floor.

It slips past feet and rucksacks. It **bumps** against a pair of trainers.

A boy, Hari, sees the book and picks it up.

Death Sentence, he reads. *A horror story?*

Hari flips through the pages, hoping to find a picture. Nothing.

Page after page is blank.

"You have a diary?" asks his friend Charlie.

1070, 754/JF

She leans over the seat behind Hari.

"Not mine," says Hari. "I think it's a horror story."

"Like Stephen King?" says Charlie. "I love him!"

Finally, Hari turns to the page with the single sentence.

"What does that mean?" asks Charlie, leaning further over the seat.

The two friends read the sentence together.

They both disappear.

The book continues to slide along the floor.

It **bumps** into more feet.

And **each time**, another hand picks it up.

And **each time**, another person disappears.

Barnaby stops talking to his friends.

He looks around at the bus.

"It feels different today," he says to Jenna and the others.

"It feels **cold**," Jenna says.

And lonely, Barnaby thinks. *I don't remember having the bus all to ourselves before.*

"Oh, look," says Jenna. "Somebody's **dropped** a book."

Chapter 3

STARING

"There aren't any words," says Jenna.

"It's someone's diary," says the other girl, Michelle.

"Oh, here's a **sentence**," says Jenna.

Barnaby **grabs** the book from her. "No," he says. "I don't think you should."

Jenna laughs and stares at him. "What's wrong with you, B?" she asks.

Michelle hugs herself. "I don't think you should read it either."

"What's that you've got there?" booms a voice.

It is the driver. He **stares** at them in his rear view mirror. He stares hard.

The bus stops at a red light.

"It's boring up here," the driver says, and gives an odd laugh. "Why don't you guys tell me a story? Or why don't you read that book you've got?"

"Um, I don't really want to," says Jenna.

The driver stands up and faces the pupils.

"I think **you** should," he says.

Chapter 4

LAST LOOK

BANG! BANG!

Someone **pounds** on the front door of the bus. A young man climbs on to the bus.

He is dressed in dark blue leather.

Dark glasses shield his eyes.

"Not you!" shouts the driver.

The driver runs down the aisle and grabs the book from Barnaby.

He finds the page with the sentence.

Then he turns and shoves the page in the young man's face.

"Read it!" he screams. "Read it!"

The young man in blue raises a hand towards the book.

The bus lurches from side to side.

The pupils scream as they fall into the aisle.

Wind **screeches** through the windows and rips the book apart.

The driver floats above the floor.

With a horrible ripping sound, he is
pulled through a window and disappears.

"Busted," the man in blue says quietly.

The seats are full of pupils once more.

Adam looks up at the strange young man.

"Who – who are you?" Adam asks.

The man in blue pulls out a white cane from his jacket.

He taps it before him as he finds his way back to the front door.

"Just a librarian," says the man.

"I've read a lot of books about magic," says Barnaby.

"But I never **saw** that coming."

The Blue Librarian smiles.

"Luckily for me, I never see it coming,"
he says, lifting his dark glasses.

The man has no eyes.

Then he steps out of the bus.

GLOSSARY

cane – wooden or plastic stick that helps a person to walk. A person who is blind often uses a special white cane to help feel what's around them.

disappears – suddenly goes out of sight

etched – drawn or cut into a tough surface using a sharp object

grimly – done in a serious, gloomy and unpleasant way

lurches – moves in an unsteady, jerking motion

odd – strange or difficult to understand

private – not meant to be shared with others

shield – cover or protect something

shoves – pushes roughly

sneers – smiles in a mean or hateful way

DISCUSSION QUESTIONS

1. Bus rides can be boring or exciting or mysterious. What is the strangest thing that has ever happened to you while riding on a bus, or on your way to school?

2. Why do you think Barnaby doesn't want Jenna to read the book? Remember the magic book that Barnaby mentions at the beginning of the story? Do you think that has anything to do with what happens to the pupils on the bus?

3. The Death Sentence is never revealed in the story, but it makes dozens of pupils disappear. Do you think words are powerful? Can words affect what happens to our lives?

WRITING PROMPTS

1. How did the dark book get on the bus? Write a paragraph describing what you think happened.

2. The story ends with the destruction of the evil book, but what happens next? Do the pupils walk to school? Does the bus driver reappear? Does the Blue Librarian appear again? Write down what happens next.

3. The hero in this book is the Blue Librarian. He has several special abilities and powers. Make a list of the ones you can discover in the story. Write about which special powers you wish you had.